Lost Property

*Pat Thomson and
Caroline Crossland*

Collins

Look out for more *Jets* from Collins

To the real Mrs Etheridge and the real Alex

First published by A & C Black Ltd in 1995
Published by Collins in 1995
10 9 8 7 6 5 4
Collins is an imprint of HarperCollins*Publishers* Ltd,
77–85 Fulham Palace Road, Hammersmith, London W6 8JB

ISBN 0 00 675098-2

Text © Pat Thomson 1995
Illustrations © Caroline Crossland 1995

The author and the illustrator assert the moral right
to be identified as the author and the illustrator of the work.
A CIP record for this title is available from the British Library.

Printed in Great Britain by
Clays Ltd, St Ives plc

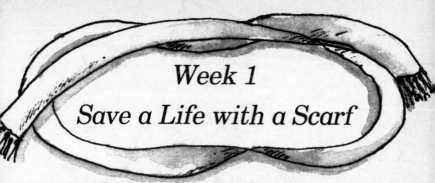

Week 1
Save a Life with a Scarf

It was Friday, the last day of the school week. Alex had brought Mrs Etheridge a letter from home. His mother had already told him what the letter said. It was about the same thing she had moaned about last week. And the week before. And the one before that.

At break, Alex's friend, Tom, came to tell him that Mrs Etheridge wanted to see him.

It's about this letter, Alex.

From my mum?

"The Findings"
Lostwithiel

Dear Mrs Etheridge,
            Would you be
kind enough to make sure
Alex looks in the Lost Property
box before he comes home
today? I can't find his new
scarf anywhere. He may
have left it at school. So
sorry to have to trouble you.
            Yours sincerely,
                  Alex's Mum.

Mrs Etheridge was waiting for an explanation so Alex thought he had better begin at the beginning.

'It was a really useless scarf, Mrs Etheridge,' he said. 'Fancy having to go to school in a long, white scarf! I thought everyone would laugh at me. I could tell that Dad didn't like it much, either.'

'But I didn't take it home again and that's the problem.'

Alex tried to explain.

You see Sue and Rosemary were practising at being doctors.

They wanted to operate on Tom, but he wasn't very keen.

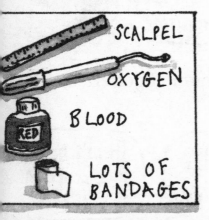

SCALPEL

OXYGEN

BLOOD

RED

LOTS OF BANDAGES

They collected some hospital equipment.

But what they really needed was a good, long bandage.

'That's where my scarf went,' said Alex. 'It was just right for a bandage and I didn't really want it anyway.'

Mrs Etheridge remembered that one of the other teachers had been talking about Tom Lister hopping around the playground, dressed as a mummy.

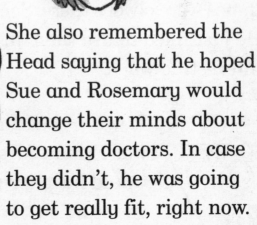

She also remembered the Head saying that he hoped Sue and Rosemary would change their minds about becoming doctors. In case they didn't, he was going to get really fit, right now.

7

'This is all very well, but I'm going to have to explain the whole story to your mother,' sighed Mrs Etheridge.

You will take extra care, won't you?

I won't lose anything Mrs Etheridge.

After all, thought Alex, he didn't actually lose things very often. The things were always there. Somewhere. He just liked to use them in interesting ways.

It was a good thing it was Friday. Mrs Etheridge would have forgotten about the scarf by next week.

Week 2
Have You Seen a Hamster in a Hat?

Alex had a good weekend. He didn't even have to stop to go shopping as Mum was busy.

A letter had come from Great-Gran saying she hoped to pay them a visit in a week or two. This had reminded Mum of all the things that Great-Gran had knitted for them. She hadn't seen them recently so she started searching through drawers and cupboards.

Alex and Dad were enjoying the peace and quiet until Mum called down the stairs to them.

Where's that sweater Great-Gran knitted for you?

Oh, no!

And where's your lovely woolly hat, Alex?

Oh, help!

So, on Monday, Alex took a second letter to Mrs Etheridge.

"The Findings"
Lostwithiel

Dear Mrs Etheridge,
I'm sorry to have to mention lost property again but I don't suppose there's any sign of Alex's woolly hat? It matched the scarf we ...ere looking for last week

'Great-Gran is a terrible knitter,' said Alex. 'She likes to use up odd bits of wool in interesting ways. Everything she knits turns out to be very colourful but the wrong size. A little while ago, she sent us all presents. You should have seen them!'

11

'Alex,' Mrs Etheridge interrupted,
'I don't need the history of the hat.
I just want to hear where it is now.'

'I was just coming to that,' said Alex.

I had the idea when you showed us the new hamsters.

You said they needed a soft, warm bed, and I had the very thing.

They seemed to like it very much.

Mrs Etheridge agreed. It might be better if Great-Gran never found out about the hat. But she still had to explain it to Alex's mum.

'Now look, Alex,' she said, 'I'm going to ask someone to help you keep an eye on your things. I'm sure Holly will do it.'

Why me?

I didn't ask you to.

Holly did try. She followed Alex around, reminding him about everything.

...and your pencil, rubber, ruler, lunch, P.E. kit.

You'll make a good mum, you will.

But Alex didn't really need to be reminded of things. No one had yet worked out that Alex's problem wasn't forgetting things, it was having brilliant ideas.

And Mrs Etheridge was about to learn about another one.

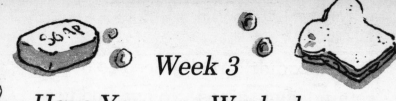

Week 3

Have You ever Washed your Face with a Sandwich?

As the next week went by, Alex became rather fed up with Holly. He felt he had one mum at school as well as one at home. She wouldn't leave him alone for a moment. Nevertheless, even she couldn't prevent the next disaster and on Friday, Alex brought a third letter from home.

"The findings"
Lostwithiel.

Dear Mrs Etheridge,

You were quite right to suggest we should forget about the hat, but we do have another little problem. I know it sounds unlikely, but I have discovered Alex's face cloth is missing.

I just wondered—

'It's quite simple.' Alex was getting used to explaining. 'You know Great-Gran is coming to pay us a visit? Mum has been busy cleaning *everything*, including me. She looked at my neck and sent me straight to the bathroom.

'But where does your face cloth come into all this?' asked Mrs Etheridge.

'I found something much more important to use it for,' said Alex.

It was when we did the 'Growing Things' project.

You said we could either choose to do 'Spring' for drama,

keep a record of everyone's height,

or bring something to grow mustard and cress on. That's where my face cloth came in useful.

Mrs Etheridge began to feel slightly
dizzy. She went over to the 'Growing
Things' display and had a look.

Everyone crowded
round. The missing
face cloth looked
like a little
green meadow.

GROWING THINGS

'It grew so well because of all the
dirt on it,' said Tom, admiringly.

Yuk!
I resign.

'Oh dear,' said Mrs Etheridge. 'Now I'll have to find someone else to help you. Perhaps Tom would be the right person. He's a good friend of yours, Alex. You and Tom work together and try to be more responsible about your belongings. We can't afford to have anything else go missing.'

'Don't worry about a thing, Mrs Etheridge. I'll take care of Alex,' said Tom.

Mrs Etheridge didn't look too hopeful. She sighed, picked up her pen and began another letter to Alex's mum.

Week 4
The First Mixing Bowl on the Moon

The following week started smoothly. Alex was making a special effort because Mrs Etheridge had promised the class they could do cookery. Alex really liked cookery. His mum had never seen anything he had cooked because he always ate it all up on the way home from school. This time, however, he had Tom – and Tom was taking his duties very seriously.

Have you remembered your apron?

I've got one of Dad's old shirts.

At the end of the day Tom made sure the coconut-ice fingers went straight home. Mum was delighted until, a few days later, she discovered not everything Alex had borrowed had been returned.

On Friday, Alex took another letter to school.

"The Findings"
Lostwithiel.

Dear Mrs Etheridge, The last time Alex did some cooking, he took my plastic mixing bowl to school and I haven't seen it since...

'No problem, no problem,' said Alex. 'It's in the cloakroom.'

'In the cloakroom?' Mrs Etheridge sat down heavily on her chair. 'Tell me more,' she said.

'Well, the week when we were doing cookery, you were also reading us that really good story,' Alex began.

'You always break off at a really
exciting part and then we act it out
in the playground. This time, it
didn't go completely right.'

We were playing at space
stories in the
playground.

We even made our own
space ship.

Then Tom brought this
really brilliant space
suit to school.

So I had to be the alien.

'I'm sure the paint will wash off. I fixed the feelers with sticky tape. It's a good idea, isn't it?'

Alex was full of good ideas. Mrs Etheridge had to admit that.

Tom beamed. 'Alex hasn't lost the bowl at all, has he? He was just borrowing it for one of his good ideas.'

'Perhaps you're not the best person to help Alex, after all,' Mrs Etheridge said, sternly. 'You should have made sure he took *everything* home. I think I'd better find someone else.'

'He took everything except the bowl and I'll make sure he takes that tonight. Can I have one more chance?' begged Tom.

'Well . . .' Mrs Etheridge paused and looked around the room. The rest of the class suddenly became very busy.

'All right then. One more chance. But please be more careful this time, I don't want any more letters from Alex's mum.'

Week 5
My Dad's Braces were a
Secret Weapon

It was only the Tuesday of the following week when Alex slipped into the classroom before school started, left a letter on Mrs Etheridge's desk, and slipped out again. Soon the whistle went. Alex knew that Mrs Etheridge would be reading the letter.

Tom, will you come in with me?

If I can wear my Dracula mask.

They both went in together. Mrs Etheridge was standing with the letter in her hand, looking quite flustered.

This is getting embarrassing.

"The Findings". Lostwithiel.

Dear Mrs Etheridge,

What a nuisance our family must be, but I'm afraid something else is lost. I hardly like to mention it, but my husband's braces are missing...

'It's true that we had a little trouble over the weekend,' Alex decided to get his story in first. 'Mum and Dad went out for the evening, you see. They were all dressed up, but Dad's trousers were a bit baggy.'

'I suppose,' said Mrs Etheridge, 'you know all about the braces?'

'It just so happens that I do,' confessed Alex. 'They aren't lost, though, are they Tom?'

'No they aren't,' confirmed Tom.
'They are somewhere being useful.'

'I'm trying to explain,' said Alex.
'You see, I was trying to tell Tom
about the Roman army but he was
in a bad mood.'

Their army was the best in the world in those days.

They had a brilliant army with brilliant machines.

I told Tom I could make something from Roman times that really worked.

The catapult really worked.

Mrs Etheridge gulped. She
remembered the ballista. She had
taken the whole class into the
playground to see it work.

She had praised it.
She had even taken
photographs of it.
She hadn't noticed
the braces.

After all, the last thing
anyone would look for
on a Roman weapon
would be Alex's dad's
braces. She began to
feel a little guilty,
nevertheless, and
that made her cross.

'I don't think you've been much use, Tom. I shall have to find someone more responsible to help Alex.'

Alex and Tom stared in amazement. It was Amy, the tidiest girl in the class. Mrs Etheridge couldn't believe it, either.

'Oh, would you, Amy? How kind! I'm sure everything will be much better with you in charge of Alex.'

Mrs Etheridge was smiling again. She was a good teacher. She never gave up hope.

Alex got right through to Thursday with Amy's help. At the end of the day she checked his tray. Then she followed him out of the classroom into the cloakroom to check his peg. He forgot nothing and Amy was very nice to him and didn't fuss like Holly.

Alex is doing very well, Mrs Etheridge.

What a treasure you are, Amy!

What poor Amy didn't know was that she was already too late. Alex's next big problem had started the week before. By Thursday morning, everyone knew about it.

This is too much, Alex.

"The Findings"
Lostwithiel.

Dear Mrs Etheridge,
It's me again, I'm afraid. Your explanation of what happened to my husband's braces makes me think that Alex may have found a use for something else I have lost. My tights have disappeared. I don't suppose it's possible...

The whole class gathered round as Alex tried to explain what his mum's tights were doing in school. This time, he did look a little guilty.

It had all started, it seemed, at the same time as his mum and dad went out for the evening.

'I went over to Tom's for the night.'

'And my mum let us stay up to watch a film,' added Tom.

'It was about some men who robbed a bank,' continued Alex. 'After a long chase, the police caught them just as they were about to leave the country.' He could remember the film well, it had been very exciting.

The next day, we were playing bank robbers at break.

We needed stocking masks but Mum only wears tights.

It was a bit of a nuisance, trying to keep together,

but it was all right until we ran in different directions.

'There's not much to take back to Mum.'

Alex went over to the paint
cupboard and took something out.
The class stared at the brown rags
with red and blue blobs on them.

Then they gasped. Alex had used
the remains of his mum's tights to
wipe the brushes on.

Amy nearly fainted.

I can't go on,
Mrs Etheridge.
I'm sorry but
I really can't!

'I'm not sure I can go on much longer, either,' said Mrs Etheridge, grimly. 'How on earth am I going to explain this to your mother? First the braces, now the tights. There's nothing more to be done,' Mrs Etheridge decided, 'from now on, it's up to the whole class to keep an eye on Alex. I'm holding you all responsible.'

The class were not happy.

IT'S NOT FAIR!

'Nor is writing all these letters to Alex's mum,' said Mrs Etheridge, crossly.

So that's that!

Week 7
We Draw a Veil over this Chapter

During the next week, there was a
terrible outbreak of losing things.
The whole class were so busy
fussing over Alex that they kept
misplacing their own things. And
many of them spent the week
finding things which weren't
really lost.

Where's my hair ribbon?

It was here a minute ago.

Has Alex lost this, Mrs Etheridge?

Is it likely, Garry?

Alex was being particularly careful. He was enjoying the special Green Week at school and he didn't want anything to go wrong.

Whenever he needed anything from home, he was careful to ask if it was all right to take it.

Can I take these?

He even asked permission before he took the used cans for the collection.

Dad said there were some old
gardening books in the attic which
Mrs Etheridge might find useful,
and Alex went up to look.
But while he was poking about, he
found a long, white dress in a
plastic cover.

The dress wasn't very interesting
but there was a useful bit of net
over the dress.

And his mum didn't seem to want it
when she saw it in his bag.

Mum said that was fine. She had changed all their net curtains for blinds, years ago. It was true that there had been a strange little circle of flowers on the net but Alex never understood his mum's decorating ideas, anyway.

Never mind, that bit of net was going to be really useful.

Then Alex had some bad luck. Mum went into the attic. She came down and spoke to Alex. There was a bit of an explosion.

She wrote another letter.

I don't believe it! This is the seventh!

You must be getting to know her quite well

"The Findings" Lostwithiel.

Dear Mrs Etheridge,

You and I have a lot in common. We both have to put up with Alex. Could you please see that he brings home my wedding veil? Yes, I do mean wedding veil. It is very old, of course, but of sentimental value. I can't think why he brought it to school but...

'Your mum's wedding veil?' gasped Amy.

'Tell us, Alex,' said Mrs Etheridge, 'why you brought it to school. We are all waiting.'

47

'It's quite simple,' said Alex.

It was during our Green Week.

I wanted to bring something for the new school pond.

I didn't know what to bring. Then I had a brilliant idea.

Frog spawn! Our neighbour had lots. That net was brilliant to catch it in.

'I've still got it. Mum can have it back if she wants, only it's a bit green and mouldy now.'

Mrs Etheridge sat down on her chair. 'I'm not sure I shall make it to the end of term if I have to write any more letters.'

Ask your mum to come and see me.

She's very busy. Great-Gran's coming next week.

Mrs Etheridge didn't say anything else but she was a bit snappy and the rest of the class blamed Alex.

It's your fault, Alex.

Why can't you look after your things?

You're dead stupid.

You have the brains of a pea.

He's already lost his brain.

Why don't you get lost, Alex?

'Never mind,' said Tom. 'You can't help having good ideas. It's only two more weeks to the holidays. I don't expect anything else will happen now.'

He was wrong. There was just a little more to come.

Week 8
My Great-Granny was a Dinosaur

Alex tried to be invisible during the next week. Mrs Etheridge was about to start writing the end of term reports and everyone, especially Alex, was trying to stay out of trouble.

Fortunately, there was a lot to finish off before then and that kept most people quiet.

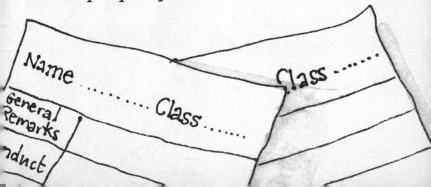

Great-Gran came to stay for the week and Alex found she wasn't half as fussy as he had expected. She never mentioned the hat or Dad's sweater although she was knitting something mysterious in purple and pink.

She even came to school and had a little chat with Mrs Etheridge who invited her to talk about what school was like when Great-Gran was young.

In fact, Alex had a lovely time
during Great-Gran's visit. She liked
the same television programmes as
he did, and she took Alex to see
a film and then to have a hamburger.

Alex's mum didn't
like him to have too
many hamburgers
but Gran said she
loved them. They
were nice and easy
to eat.

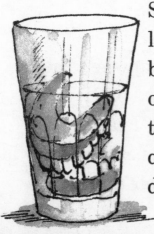

She told him to always
look after his teeth
because having false
ones was a great
trouble. Alex was
astonished to find she
didn't wear hers at night.

That gave him an idea.

He had it on Wednesday when the class were working hard on their models. They had been learning about prehistoric times and were making a world for their dinosaurs to roam in.

54

Apart from Tom, the rest of the class weren't really speaking to him so Alex worked on his own. He could see, however, that some of the class were quite impressed with his dinosaur. It was working out really well but Alex wasn't completely satisfied. There was something wrong with it.

By Thursday, he had solved the problem.

By Friday, Mrs Etheridge had another letter.

'It was like this,' said Alex, and all the class groaned.

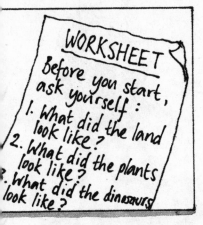

When we did our model of prehistoric times,

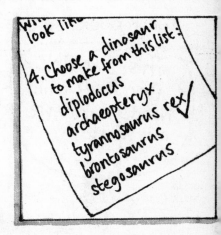

I chose to make a tyrannosaurus rex!

Then we put the model together.

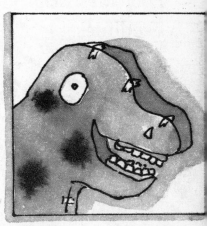

My tyrannosaurus looked quite boring until I put the teeth in.

'If you've finished with the display, Mrs Etheridge, I'll take Great-Gran's teeth back.'

Poor Mrs Etheridge imagined the headlines.

'I will write to your mother at once,' declared Mrs Etheridge, 'and explain everything.'

'I hope your mother realises that I didn't ask you to bring all those things.'

'You really must be more careful
with your belongings.'

'It must be catching, Alex. I can't find it anywhere and I need it to write your end of term reports.'

Mrs Etheridge looked in her bag, then her desk, then she stopped and thought.

* P.S. What do you think?